# Rodeo Clown

## D.L. Winchester

Winchester Horror Publishing

For the Bullfighters

# 1

Matt McAllister leaned against a railing, watching the bullfighter get into his barrel. Beyond him, the sun was setting over the Arizona desert, lighting up the sky in a kaleidoscope of orange and pink.

*Bullfighters,* he thought. *They'll always be rodeo clowns to me.*

He smiled. The traditions were part of what he loved about rodeos, along with traveling around the west with his best friend, and the beauty of sunsets like the one tonight.

Red letters on the white-painted grandstands told him he was in Bisbee, another small town on the rodeo circuit. Johnny Cash blared over the loudspeakers as Garrett Nichols walked past him.

"You ready?" Matt asked, following him toward the chutes.

"It's just ol' *Staycation*," Garrett replied. "I can get seventy points on him with my eyes closed."

"Do me a favor and try that." Matt grinned, slapping his friend on the back and silently cursing his own luck.

He'd been hoping to draw *Staycation*, the easiest ride on the livestock roster. Matt had gone eight rodeos without a qualifying ride, sixteen bulls, no points, a streak that had to end soon. His bank account was bare, and if his luck didn't change, he'd have to dip into his savings to stay on the circuit.

And his savings wouldn't last long.

Garrett dropped aboard *Staycation,* the animal restless in the chute, and Matt helped him get settled. The gate behind him lurched, where Matt's own ride was waiting. *Airborne,* two thousand pounds of mean with a dash of pure bullshit. Of the twelve animals for tonight's performance, *Airborne* had been the one Matt didn't want to draw.

So of course he had.

The PA system cackled to life. *"Next up, Garrett Nichols on Staycation!"*

Garrett made his final adjustments, cinching the rope around his glove. He nodded once, and the gate flew open.

*"Here we go, folks!"*

Through the gate, Matt watched *Staycation* dip his head as he moved into a tight turn. Coming out of the turn, the bull leapt once, twice, punctuating each leap with a kick of his legs. Garrett dug his spurs into the animal's flanks, right hand in the air.

*Staycation* wasn't done. He moved into another tight turn, then planted his front feet and kicked the air as Garrett held on. The bull started into another turn, then the horn sounded eight seconds.

A qualifying ride.

The pickup men spurred their horses into action as the clowns—no, bullfighters—worked *Staycation*. Garrett slid off the animal's back to the arena floor, and one of the riders moved between him and *Staycation* in case the bull wanted to come discuss the ride. Garrett climbed up on the gate, waving his hat to the cheering crowd.

*"Our second qualifying ride of the night,"* the announcer called as the judges quickly put in their scores. Up to fifty points each for the rider and the bull.

The riders guided *Staycation* out the exit gate as Matt put on his helmet and looked down into the chute where *Airborne* was waiting. The bull lifted its head, the black eyes showing nothing.

*The scores are in,* the announcer called. *Garrett Nichols on Staycation with a seventy-eight point ride!*

Another wave of cheers broke out as Matt positioned himself on *Airborne.* He could feel the beast's raw power between his legs, his own heart racing as it pumped adrenaline through his body. Matt felt beads of sweat forming under his helmet, where he wouldn't be able to reach them until after the ride.

Man versus bull.

The ultimate thrill.

Truth was, he'd do this for free. The pulsing adrenaline, the roar of the crowd, it was an addiction, an unbeatable high.

Hands came in, helping him position the strap and watching as he wrapped the rope around his glove. Someone slapped the top of his helmet.

"Good luck," Matt heard Garrett say.

For a moment, he looked through the gate at the arena's dirt floor and the sunset beyond it.

Then he nodded and the gate swung open.

★★★

Garrett grinned as he helped Matt load his gear into his truck. "Two seconds!"

"Two point eight," Matt replied, shaking his head.

"Hell, you were airborne for half that," Garrett shot back.

"Don't say that word," Matt cautioned, slamming the tailgate closed.

"What? Hell?"

"You know damn well which one I meant."

Garrett wrapped his arm around Matt's shoulders. "Cheer up, pal. It's dance night, and I'm sure the ladies of Bisbee, Arizona will be lining up to help heal a wounded cowboy's pride." He stepped away from Matt, a wicked grin on his face. "That's assuming you can make it more than two point eight seconds in the sack!"

Matt snorted. "Unlike some people, I've never had a problem with that."

"So come on. Let's have a good time, get laid, and in the morning we can ride out to wherever the hell our next stop is."

"Pecos, Texas," Matt said. "About an eight hour drive."

"It's Saturday night. We don't have to be there until Wednesday morning. Maybe we'll stop in El Paso for a couple days, try to snap you out of this funk." Garrett elbowed Matt playfully. "Or depending on how tonight goes, maybe we'll spend a couple extra days in Bisbee."

"Do you mind? I'm trying to be miserable here," Matt said, but he was smiling.

"It's going about as well as your bull riding has been lately," Garrett grinned back. "Come on, what's the worst that could happen?"

"We come back next year and get introduced to little Garrett."

"What? You're not worried about little Matt?"

Matt grunted. "I think *Airborne* took care of that for me."

Garrett laughed and grabbed his arm. "Come on, so what have you got to lose?"

Matt paused for a moment, and Garrett rolled his eyes. "Come on, man. I've told you a thousand times. My sister's out living her best life while you're too damn afraid to ask her out. If you're gonna be a chicken, you should at least have *some* fun."

"I don't know, man. I really like her. It just feels like I should be some kind of loyal, you know?"

Garrett rolled his eyes. "You aren't even dating her yet. To her, you're just her brother's awkward friend." He punched Matt's shoulder. "Enjoy being young, dude. Maybe putting yourself out there will help you work up the nerve to do something about your crush."

A sigh. "Maybe you're right."

"So come on! Tonight, Bisbee is our oyster!"

# 2

Pecos, a dusty oilfield Texas town located on its namesake river, staked its claim as home to the world's first rodeo just after its founding in the late 1800s, a title only a few other places would ever dispute.

There was one thing for sure—it was hot as hell at the end of June, with daytime temperatures soaring into the triple digits.

"Thank God this place is air conditioned," Matt said as they entered the town's museum, located in an old hotel by the railroad tracks.

"I can't believe you made me leave Bisbee for this," Garrett said. "That chick couldn't get enough of me. It's not my fault you struck out."

Matt rolled his eyes and paid their admission. "It wouldn't have been so bad if you were at her place, but in our shared room, it was a little much."

"Whatever." They went into a room decorated as an old west saloon. "We could be living it up in El Paso right now. They've got air conditioning there too."

Matt shook his head. He liked Garrett's company, but he tended to live a little too fast and loose for his liking. "You know I like getting to town early, check out the local sights before we start competing."

"Shit, I like local sights too. Senoritas in bikinis by the pool…"

"Hey, it says a guy was shot and killed here," Matt interrupted, pointing to a brass plaque on the floor.

"That's morbid," Garrett said, coming over for a look. "You reckon he was a famous outlaw or something?"

Matt shrugged. "Probably got too close to a senorita he shouldn't have."

A laugh. "That was two years ago, and she didn't tell me she was married."

"And both times I've gone back to Alamogordo, you've decided it's time for a trip home." Matt twisted the knife with a smile.

"It's for my health," Garrett muttered as they climbed the stairs to explore the museum's upper floors.

***

They finally came out in the museum gift shop.

"What is it with Pecos and cantaloupes?" Garrett asked, studying a T-shirt with *Melon-Dollar Town* printed on it.

"Something about the soil around here, makes them extra sweet," Matt replied, looking at the book selection. "There was an exhibit about it upstairs."

"You say that like you thought I was looking at the exhibits too," Garrett replied, picking up a bowl in the shape of half a cantaloupe.

"There was some interesting stuff," Matt said, picking out a couple books and walking toward the register. As he passed a display case, he looked down. "Wow," he said.

"What? Cantaloupe earrings?" Garrett walked over.

"Yeah, man, your birthday's coming up, seems like the kind of present you get the cowboy that has everything," Matt cracked. "Look at that ring."

Garrett followed Matt's gaze to a tarnished silver ring with a band of turquoise around the middle. Etched into a silver spot in the center was a pair of bull horns.

"You want to wear a ring?" Garrett asked. "Bad idea. Chicks will think you're married."

Matt punched his shoulder. "I think it looks lucky. And with the streak I'm on, I could use a little luck."

Garrett whistled at the price tag next to the ring. "Seventy-seven bucks. That actually sounds promising."

Matt waved to the girl manning the gift shop register. She was young, even compared to his twenty-two. Probably a teenager working for some extra cash. "I'd like to look at this ring, please."

She walked over and unlocked the case, taking out the ring and handing it to Matt. He slid it on his right ring finger.

It was a perfect fit.

"Yeah, I'll take it," Matt said, sliding it off and handing it to the girl. "Do you know anything about it?"

She shrugged. "I just work the register while school's out. You'd have to ask my mom, but she's out helping set up for the rodeo."

"No big deal," Matt said, pulling out his wallet and paying cash for the ring and books. The girl put it in a jewelry box, and Matt put it in his pocket.

Garrett slapped him on the back as they went back out into the heat. "You better hope that ring is as lucky as you think it is, because I'm feeling lucky too, and I don't need no ring to outride you."

# 3

"*REVENUER,*" MATT READ FROM the draw sheet posted outside the rodeo office. He turned to Garrett. "You ever heard of him?"

Garrett shook his head. "Must be a new bull this year."

"Who'd you draw?"

"*Governor of Pain.*" Garrett bit his lip. "I can't believe he hasn't been retired yet."

"You said that two weeks ago in Tucson, and he went and bucked my ass off,"

Matt said, moving away from the crowd around the bulletin board.

It was two hours until the evening performance and the sun still beat down on the rodeo grounds. Behind the grandstands, concession stands were being set up under tents, selling bar-b-que, fairground favorites, lemonade, and Mexican drinks like horchata and cantaloupe. Near the ticket booths, massive trailers with rodeo merchandise were waiting, with flat-screen TVs inside showing highlights from past rodeos.

Matt got a horchata, Garrett grabbed a soda, and they wandered into the wooden grandstands. Taking a seat in one of the few boxes in the shade, they watched as the arena slowly came to life.

★★★

Three hours later, as they sat out the barrels for barrel racing, they made their way down to the bucking chutes, where they grabbed their gear and checked the roster again.

"Looks like I'm up first," Matt said.

"Second-to-last," Garrett replied. "I'll still be in the showers when you're sitting in the truck wishing you had the balls to text my sister."

"Maybe not," Matt replied. "I've been thinking that maybe you're right, I do need to live a little. If things are meant to be with Gabi, they'll work out, and if not…" He shrugged. "Chicks dig cowboys."

Garrett groaned. "Great. More competition."

"Tough luck, old buddy." Matt grinned, holding up his hand so Garrett could see the ring. "Maybe I've got all the luck now."

Garrett rolled his eyes. "Come on, you turkey."

★★★

As the last barrel racer disappeared out of the arena, Matt looked down at *Revenuer* in the first chute. He looked young, but youth could be dangerous. Sometimes it was better to have an older bull you knew a little bit about than a young one who could do anything on you. This one was calm in the chute, with a tan coat and dull black eyes. It barely moved when Matt climbed into the chute and began positioning his rope.

"It might be a dud," Garrett said from the platform. "I ain't never seen a bull that calm in the chute before."

"Reminds me of *Plainsman,*" Matt said, wrapping the end of the rope around his hand.

"Hell, even he had some life to him." Garrett shook his head. "You're probably going to end up with a re-ride. Hope you're in the mood to ride twice tonight." He stepped away from the chute.

Matt looked through the gate. More folks had trickled in as the night went on and the temperature dropped. The stands were full now, with the announcer, on horseback, playing their cheerleader.

"These cowboys will do better the louder you are," he said.

Matt took a deep breath and nodded.

The gate slammed open.

★★★

*Revenuer* was not a dud.

He turned out of the gate and immediately dropped his face to the dirt, kicking his legs high and almost throwing Matt over his horns. Matt barely managed to right himself before the bull leaped across the arena once, twice, then a third time with a hard twist thrown in while Matt spurred the animal for all he was worth.

*No you don't,* Matt thought as the bull went into a turn. Right hand in the air, he hung on.

*How long has it been?* It felt like eight seconds.

It felt like a lifetime.

The bull rocketed into another leap, then kicked its legs before powering into another turn in the opposite direction than the last one.

"Holy fuck!" Matt yelled, knowing the profanity would be lost in the roar of the crowd.

The horn finally sounded, and Matt grabbed the rope with his free hand. *Revenuer* straightened out as the pickup men moved in to get Matt.

Then Matt saw him.

A clown in turquoise and black appeared in front of the bull. *Revenuer* slammed on the brakes, almost throwing Matt over the horns into the clown. Matt managed to hang on, then used the sudden stop to slide down to the arena floor.

He ran for the chute's open gate as the bull took a victory lap, thundering to the far end of the arena before the pickup men managed to turn him for the exit chute.

"Here you go." One of the bullfighters handed Matt his hat and bull rope.

"Thanks." Matt scanned the arena, looking for the turquoise getup. "Who was the fucking clown?"

His eyes narrowed. "Son, you know we're called bullfighters now and we've definitely saved enough asses over the years to earn your respect."

"Not you," Matt said quickly. "The idiot in turquoise."

"Ain't no one out here but me and Todd." He gestured to the other bullfighter, wearing orange and silver and talking to the barrel man. "You sure you didn't hit your head?"

Matt looked around the arena again, confused. He knew he'd seen a rodeo clown dressed up like they used to, in black pants and a turquoise shirt, with black suspenders. He thought a little more. Yeah. He'd had black circles painted around his eyes, turquoise paint on the rest of his face, and a black cowboy hat. Definitely not one of these two bullfighters.

"You okay, kid?" the bullfighter asked again.

"Yeah, I'm fine."

He slapped Matt's back. "Good ride, son."

With the bull out of the arena, Matt hopped off the gate and stepped back to look at the video board mounted behind the chutes. It was showing a replay of his ride while the judges got the scores in.

Watching, Matt felt good. The bull had done its job, and he'd managed to stay on the full eight seconds. This should be good news.

*The scores are in*, the announcer called over the PA system. *Matt McAllister… On Revenuer… With a score of ninety-three!*

Matt grabbed his hat and hurled it into the air. Ninety-three! That was a career best for him, a score that would definitely earn him some money at the end of the night, and a sign his luck might finally be turning.

*Who cares about the fucking clown?* he thought as he sauntered off the arena floor. *With a score like that, that clown can do whatever he wants.*

# 4

THE TRUCK flew down the interstate, brown mesas on both sides and not much else to look at between Pecos and Sonora, their next stop.

"Let me get this straight," Garrett said. "Not only do you get a ninety-three point ride out of a bull no one's ever heard of before, but you miss my ride because some local floozie decides she wants to put out for the big rodeo star?"

Matt laughed. "How many times have you left me alone to ride because you had a chance to get laid?"

"That's my point! It's something I would do, not you!"

"And this has nothing to do with your seventy-three point ride?" Matt looked at his friend to see him squirm before turning his eyes back to the road.

"Goddamn *Governor of Pain,*" Garrett mumbled. "They should have put him out to pasture years ago."

"And don't forget you had to sleep in the truck because you struck out."

"What the fuck has gotten into you?" Garrett asked. "You're gloating. That's my job."

Matt took his right hand off the steering wheel and held it up, showing the ring. "A little luck, that's all."

"I may have to borrow that," Garrett mumbled as the truck sped down the highway.

★★★

Sonora, Texas is a small town on the western edge of the Texas hill country. If it wasn't for the interstate, it wouldn't have grown into the town it was.

The stands were already full when the rodeo started, mainly because there wasn't much else to do on a Thursday night in Sonora. Matt checked the draw and found he'd been assigned a bull named *No Comprende*. Garrett would be climbing aboard *Roughneck*.

"I grabbed a blanket for you from the souvenir stand," Matt told Garrett as they stood along the arena fence, watching the team ropers compete. "If you have to spend another night in the truck, I don't want you to be uncomfortable."

"It wasn't sleeping in the truck that bugged me," Garrett said, shaking his head. "It was when you didn't turn up until noon."

Matt shrugged. "I had to make sure she was satisfied."

"Sure." He looked around. "Tonight may be lonely again."

"Hey, if you're that concerned, I bet they'll let you curl up in the stock trailer with *Roughneck*."

"Jesus…"

***

Garrett was the first one to go that night. *Roughneck* was as rough as his name advertised, tossing Garrett three seconds into the run on a wild twist.

Finally, it was Matt's turn. Last ride of the night. He dropped into the chute, getting comfortable on the bull's back as another cowboy helped position his bull rope. Wrapping the end around his hand, he grabbed with his other hand as *No Comprende* backed into the side of the chute.

"Looks like he's full of energy," Garrett said, arriving behind them.

"Yeah." Matt took a deep breath, then looked out the gate.

The turquoise clown was standing there in the middle of the arena, grinning at him.

"Fuck," Matt cried.

"I keep telling you, the rope goes around your hand, not your dick." Garrett leaned in to see what Matt needed.

"Not here, do you see the clown? Out there in the arena?"

"What?" Garrett leaned over the bull to peer through the bars. "The bullfighters?"

"No, an honest-to-God rodeo clown, makeup and all."

Garrett shook his head and slid back. "Sure don't. You sure you're okay?"

"I may need my eyes checked," Matt muttered. He took another deep breath and nodded.

The gate flew open and *No Comprende* leaped into the arena. Matt hung on through a jump, but when the bull rolled onto a twist, he felt his center of gravity shifting.

*Crap!*

He let go of the bull rope and landed on the arena dirt. When he looked up, the bull was leaping away, but beyond it, standing by the fence at the end of the grandstand, the clown was smiling at him.

"What the fuck!"

"Language, kid," one of the bullfighters said, handing Matt his bull rope. "That was a mean twist he pulled on you."

"Yeah, got me off."

"Ain't many who could have stayed on." The bullfighter slapped him on the back, and before Matt left the arena, he looked back toward the grandstands.

The clown was gone.

# 5

Matt was sitting on the tailgate of his truck when Garrett appeared, followed by two girls.

"Hey dude, this is Mary and Macy," he grinned, gesturing to the girls. They were obviously sisters, but not identical. One was blonde and lean, and the other had brown hair and a little weight on her. Matt knew what Garrett had in mind before he said it.

"Macy and I want to get to know each other, but she didn't want to leave Mary alone." He nodded toward the dark haired girl. "So I told her I had a friend I could introduce her to."

Matt slid off the tailgate. "Nice to meet you."

"Likewise." She smiled at him.

"Well, now that you two are acquainted, bye!" Garrett took Macy's hand and led her away giggling.

Mary looked at Garrett. "So, what now?"

"What do you mean?" he asked.

"Well, I don't usually do this, so I don't know what happens next. Macy's the wild child of the family," she explained.

Matt grinned. "Pull up some tailgate."

She sat down next to him, and he smiled at her. "So if Macy's the wild child, what do you do for fun?"

"Study, mostly. I'm going for my PhD in neuroscience."

Matt laughed. "What a coincidence, I think I'm going crazy."

"What do you mean?" She reached out and took his hand.

He sighed. "I mean, for the last two nights, I've seen something no one else has."

"Okay, that's definitely weird. Did you fall on your head or something?"

He shook his head. "No, I feel normal, except for seeing the damn clown."

Now Mary laughed.

"What's funny?"

"Of all the things you could hallucinate, a clown is definitely a weird one."

"Thank you, I think," he said.

"It's not a bad thing," she said. "And honestly, if that's all that's happening, you probably aren't crazy. There's just something involving a clown in your life that you need to resolve."

"You think so?"

"I hope so," she said, reaching over to undo the pearl snaps on his shirt. "Though it wouldn't be the first time I fucked a crazy person."

"You're kinda bold," Matt said, letting her slide the shirt off him.

"Yeah, usually I get better results with my shy and innocent act," she smiled. "But you didn't bite, and for some reason, it's turning me on."

He leaned in and kissed her, sliding his hand under her shirt to grope her breast over her bra. "I can be bold too," he whispered.

"Good."

★★★

Garrett looked like he hadn't slept at all when he climbed into the truck the next morning.

"Good night?" Matt asked him.

Garrett just glared at him. Finally, he shook his head. "Macy drove us out to the local lovers lane, and we got in the backseat. Kissing, exploring, the usual. I'd just gotten her bra off when a car pulls in behind us and the red and blues start flashing."

"Oh shit," Matt laughed.

"Turns out, Macy is eighteen, a rising senior in high school, and she missed her curfew. Apparently one of the boys in town was upset a cowboy was going to make time with the local sweetheart, so he called the Sheriff and told him where to find us. I about had a heart attack when she called him 'daddy.'"

More laughter. "God, that's incredible!"

"Oh, it gets worse. Daddy's plenty pissed, tells Macy to get her ass home, and throws me in the back of his squad car. Takes me down to the county jail, throws me in the drunk tank, and tells me to 'think about what I've done.'"

"And did you?" Matt asked, starting the truck and pulling out of the rodeo grounds.

"Honestly, all I could think about was how soft her breast felt in my hand." Garrett grinned.

"You should have seen it," Matt said.

"What?" Garrett's brow furrowed.

"Well, instead of going home, Macy went to her sister's place to complain about how unfair her daddy was being." Matt grinned. "One thing led to another, and I'll just say those sisters are something special."

Garrett slumped down in his seat. "Come on…"

"You picked the wrong one too, man. Macy was pretty good, but Mary did some things I'd never seen before. She had pierced nipples too, I know you like those."

"Fuck my life," Garrett moaned. "I wish this was my truck so I could kick you out."

Matt laughed. "Did you need to walk awhile?"

"Fuck no." He sighed. "How come you have all the luck?"

Matt held up his right hand. "Lucky ring, dude."

# 6

They drove north through San Angelo to Sweetwater, passing through open fields of farmland before returning to the usual west Texas scrub.

Sweetwater was just another interstate town in a state full of them. Their arena was indoors, and small. For a Friday night performance, it was packed to the gills, forcing Matt and Garrett to find a place backstage to wait.

The back of the arena was a busy place, with horses and riders coming and going as staff moved livestock around. Matt had drawn a bull named *Elevator Pitch,* while Garrett would be climbing aboard *Chief Justice.*

Matt was the first of the two to ride, climbing onto the black and white beast. He was not docile in the chute, moving his body from side to side, front to back, already trying to dislodge Matt.

"Hey," Matt said, looking at Garrett. "Watch for that damn clown."

"The one only you can see?"

Matt glared at him. "Not fucking funny, man."

Garrett shrugged. "I'll see what I can see."

"Thanks." Matt finished wrapping the end of the bull rope around his hand as *Elevator Pitch* slammed into the gate, almost crushing Matt's leg.

No sense keeping this energy contained.

Matt nodded, and the gate flew open.

*Elevator Pitch* took three great bounds across the arena, dropping his head and kicking his hind legs with each leap. Matt held on as the bull turned left into a spin. Coming out of the spin, he leapt again, going back toward the chutes.

Matt managed a brief glance at the scoreboard. Five seconds. Three left.

*Elevator Pitch* made another leap, almost throwing Matt over its horns, before going into a tight turn. Matt heard the buzzer sound, and as the bull came out of the turn, slid off.

The bull stopped, looking around. Thirty feet away, a bullfighter tried to get the bull's attention.

"Hey!"

Matt looked to his right and there he was. Three feet away, waving his arms.

Matt knew he wasn't crazy now. The bull saw the clown too. Ignoring the bull-fighter, he turned, lowered his head, and charged toward Matt.

"Shit!" He dove out of the way as the bull thundered past, looking up to discover one of the pickup men had moved between him and the bull. Matt got to his feet and looked at where the rodeo clown had been.

He was gone.

"Hey, kid, get moving!" the pickup man called.

Matt ran toward the open chute as the other pickup man approached the bull, twirling a lasso to drive him toward the exit chute.

"Jesus!" Garrett grinned. "I thought that bull was going to run your ass over."

"Did you see it?" Matt gasped.

"See what?"

"The fucking clown, that's what!" Matt got up on the catwalk. "He was standing right next to me!"

Garrett shook his head. "All I saw was that bull coming at you. It did not look happy."

Matt sighed. "The damn clown was next to me. It called to the bull, got it to rush me."

"What? Are you okay, man?"

"I'm fine," Matt said, as the speakers cackled to life.

"Matt McAllister, on *Elevator Pitch*, with an eighty-eight point ride!"

Garrett shook his head. "You keep this shit up, I may have to borrow that damn lucky charm of yours." He slapped Matt on the shoulder. "Don't run off, now. The ladies can wait until I've beaten your ass on *Chief Justice*!"

★★★

The next morning, they rolled north, bound for Childress.

"You didn't make it out of the arena before someone grabbed you," Garrett grumbled in the driver's seat.

Matt grinned. "Jealous much?"

"Every girl I approached had a boyfriend," Garrett groaned. "A couple of them even threatened to whip my ass."

"Hey, maybe you could have gotten a sympathy fuck that way."

"The bulls are bad enough, man." He shook his head. "Who was that girl you ended up with anyway?"

"Danielle? Barrel racer out of East Texas. We had a grand ol' time in her hotel room."

"Figures. What's your plan after tonight?" They were heading north through Hamlin toward Childress, their last rodeo of the week.

"I'm not sure." Matt kind of wanted to look into the ring some more, but that meant the kind of boring research Garrett wouldn't be interested in, maybe even a trip back to Pecos. Sure, he could make some phone calls, but he liked actually being there to talk to people. They tended to be friendlier and more forthcoming that way.

After Childress, they'd pick up the circuit in Ruidoso, New Mexico, relatively close to Pecos. But in west Texas, relatively close was measured in hours, not miles.

"You can come home to Amarillo with me if you want. Normally I'd say I knew a couple girls who might be desperate enough to sleep with you, but the way your luck's been running, I don't think you need my help…"

Matt's phone vibrated, and he looked down to see a message from his Pecos hookup. Amanda. Thank goodness he'd put her name in his phone.

*You fucking ruined other men for me with that cock of yours. Next time you're in Pecos, I NEED to see you!*

Matt grinned. Going to Pecos just for a museum wasn't quite a good reason, but a couple of days with Amanda thrown in would make it worth the drive.

"Thanks, man, but I think I'm going back to Pecos."

"Thank God!" Garrett clapped his hands together. "Maybe the rest of us will have a chance."

# 7

Located on the northwestern edge of the hill country, Childress, Texas is at the crossroads of US-83 and US-287. A few miles from the southwest corner of Oklahoma, it's technically part of the Texas Panhandle, but also not quite. Perhaps what it's best known for is its police chief telling a group dedicated to the separation of church and state to "go fly a kite" when they requested the department remove "In God We Trust" from its patrol cars.

Small towns. You get your entertainment where you can find it.

And on Saturday night, it was at the Childress Rodeo Grounds. The arena was standing room only, with crowds filling the metal overflow bleachers and lining the fences.

"You're in a good mood," Garrett said as they pushed through the crowd.

"Yeah." Garrett's family had come down to watch, including his older sister, Gabi.

"Matt McAllister," she'd said when she saw him, looking him up and down. "You've grown up."

When she went in for a hug, she'd whispered, "I bet I can make something else grow."

Garrett watched her walk away, then shook his head. "I suppose it's a waste of breath to tell you to keep your hands off my sister?"

"After everyone in the house heard what you did with mine?" Matt grinned. "My good luck charm is on fire."

"Except that damn clown you think you keep seeing."

"Look, I see it," Matt insisted as they ducked behind the chutes. "I don't know why you can't."

"Maybe your luck has something to do with it."

Matt stopped, and looked down at the ring. Turquoise and silver. Could that be it? Maybe since Garrett didn't have the ring, that's why he couldn't see the clown.

But how to test it?

★★★

The last barrel racer rode out of the arena as Garrett settled in on *Hangman.* The black bull had a white ring around its neck, obviously the source of its name. Matt helped Garrett make his final adjustments, and just before he stepped back, slid the ring off his finger and into Garrett's vest pocket.

The crowd was on its feet, watching as the barrel man dropped into his metal hiding spot. Tonight's bullfighters, in silver and red, waited outside the chute. Garrett took a deep breath and nodded.

*Hangman* exploded out of the chute, bounding across the arena as Garrett held on. The bull's next jump added a twist, almost managing to dislodge Garrett. But he righted himself, or rather the bull did, turning into the direction Garrett was falling. Exploding into another leap, the bull turned again, then bounced two more times before the horn sounded.

And there he was.

The rodeo clown appeared in the middle of the arena as Garrett jumped off.

Garrett ran toward the chutes, but tripped and fell in the dirt.

*Hangman* stopped, the clown appearing between the bull and Garrett, waving his arms. The bull turned, saw Garrett in the dirt, and charged.

*Oh fuck.*

"Get up! Get up!" Matt yelled. Garrett looked back and exploded off the ground, breaking into a sprint, two thousand pounds of angry bovine gaining on him. Garrett jumped for the gate and Matt pulled him up, the bull curving out of the way at the last possible moment.

"Look!" Matt pointed.

The clown was still standing in the center of the arena, grinning at them while the pickup men chased the bull toward the exit chute.

The chute gate clanged shut, startling them. When they looked back into the arena, the clown was gone.

"Son of a bitch," Garrett said.

Matt reached in his pocket and took out the ring. "Believe me now?"

Garrett nodded.

***

In spite of his dangerous exit, Garrett scored a 90, beating Matt by a single point.

Gabi was waiting outside the main gate.

"Y'all going back to Amarillo tonight?" Matt asked.

"They are," Gabi said, nodding toward Garrett and her parents, loading his gear in their truck. "I'm staying over and heading to Dallas in the morning."

"Oh."

"Can you drop me off at my hotel so they can get on the road?" she asked with a sly grin.

"Sure."

Garrett walked over, shaking his head. "You two are really rubbing it in."

"Two words, bro," Gabi said. "Julie. Pearson."

Matt raised an eyebrow. "I don't think I've heard that story."

"Look at the time," Garrett said. "We really should be on the road."

"See you."

Matt and Gabi watched as Garrett walked away, then Gabi took his hand.

"Are you sure you want to do this?" Matt asked.

Gabi grinned. "Hell yes."

★★★

Her motel was less than a mile from the rodeo grounds, but they didn't make it there before the kissing started. Two red lights gave them two chances to start.

Gabi opened the door of her room and pulled him inside.

"You act like you've been waiting for this," Matt said, unbuttoning his jeans and letting them drop to the floor.

"Like I said, Matt," she pushed him against the door and grinned. "You've grown up."

He wrapped his arms around her and kissed her, sliding his hand under her shirt and moving it up to her breast. "I've always wondered what it would be like to fuck you."

Gabi grinned, stepping back and sliding out of her own jeans, then pulling her shirt over her head. She was petite, but her breasts filled her bra. Matt stared as she reached back and unhooked it, letting it fall to the floor.

"Holy fuck," Matt gasped.

"Hey," Gabi chuckled. "My eyes are up here."

"Yes, they are." Picking her up, he carried her to the bed and laid her on it. She sat up enough to slide his boxers down, letting his cock pop out.

"Mmmm." She licked her lips. "That's gonna be nice."

He laid down next to her, pulling her in for a kiss, then Gabi rolled on top, straddling him as she slid his cock inside her wet pussy.

"I bet I can ride better than you," she whispered.

Matt grinned. "God, I hope so."

# 8

MATT DIDN'T LEAVE FOR Pecos until Monday morning.

"I'd stay longer," Gabi said, kissing him goodbye. "But I have to be in Dallas for work, and frankly, I need a break."

He kissed her, putting his hands under her ass to lift her into him.

"Where are you going to be this week?" she asked.

"Ruidoso, Silver City, Santa Fe, and Hereford," he replied.

"Hmm. Maybe I'll try to catch up to you at some point."

"I'd like that."

Gabi grabbed his crotch. "I like this."

★★★

Soon after she drove away, Matt pointed his truck south. The trip to Pecos would take him six hours, putting him there an hour or so before the museum closed. If he had to, he could stay over until Tuesday, then head for Ruidoso that afternoon.

He'd just gotten on the interstate at Big Spring when his phone chimed. It was Gabi.

*Miss these yet?* She was standing in a bathroom, shirt lifted to expose her bare breasts.

*Jesus! You're gonna cause a wreck!*

A minute later, her reply came through.

*I take that as a yes ;)*

Matt shook his head. He liked having Gabi flirting with him. Matt glanced at the ring on his hand. Was it lucky? Was it worth dealing with the clown?

In the next picture, Gabi was naked in front of the mirror.

Yeah, Matt decided. This was definitely worth the clown.

\#

He climbed out of his truck at the museum in Pecos as the afternoon sun was beating down on the small town. It was quiet, you could hardly tell a rodeo had wrapped up Saturday night.

Matt removed his hat as he walked into the museum, and saw the same girl standing behind the gift shop counter.

"You're back," she said.

"I am. I wanted to ask your mom about the ring." He held up his hand.

A woman, the girl's older mirror, came around the corner. "So you're the one who bought the ring," she smiled.

"Yes ma'am."

"It's a beautiful piece. We just didn't have a place in the exhibits for it," she said.

"Is there a story behind it?" he asked.

"Oh, of course. Follow me."

He followed her through the saloon and up the stairs.

"A lot of people when their loved ones pass look at all the old junk and think, 'we'll just donate it to the museum,'" she said, leading him down the hall. "Unfortunately, we can't use most of what they offer. Our display space is limited, and the historic value is generally low. But in some cases, the donations fit the western aesthetic and can be sold in the gift shop."

"Like my ring," Matt said.

"Exactly." She stopped in a room dedicated to the rodeo. "Your ring was donated by the children of Sulema Smith. Sulema's husband was a rodeo clown, well known. He was gored by a bull at a performance and passed away. It was tragic, actually. Sulema moved home to Pecos and lived out her days here."

"And when she passed, her children thought of the museum," Matt said.

"Naturally," the director smiled. "We were able to use quite a few of the pieces they donated, actually." She walked to a nearby armoire and opened it. "This was the father's clown costume."

Matt looked inside and felt his heart stop.

Black pants.

Turquoise shirt.

Black suspenders.

Black hat.

It was the same suit his clown wore.

Fucking hell.

"Over here, I have a picture too," the director continued. "They called him 'Turquoise the Clown.'"

The picture was attached to an article. **Beloved Rodeo Clown Dies in Arena.**

*Turquoise the Clown passed away Friday, July 6, 1983, while performing at his hometown rodeo in Silver City, New Mexico…*

"This is interesting," Matt said, twisting the ring around his finger. "I didn't realize how much history the ring held."

"Turquoise left quite a legacy," the director agreed.

Matt nodded. "He left something, alright."

★★★

Matt sat on the tailgate of his truck, watching the Pecos River flow by. It was barely a river, most folks would call the trickle of water passing this bridge outside Pecos a stream.

He was looking at the ring, trying to decide what to do with it.

*It's lucky as hell. You got three great rides with it, and Garrett kicked ass at Childress with it in his pocket.*

*But that damn clown… it's out for blood! Both you and Garrett have almost ended up dead because of it.*

*Gabi. You spent two days with Gabi, and she's still flirting. You didn't even text that girl in Pecos yet, and you probably won't.*

*But you can't fuck Gabi if you're dead.*

*Maybe she'll still want you without the ring.*

*That damn clown isn't worth it.*

*Gabi is though.*

*So keep her and ditch the clown.*

Pulling the ring off his finger, he hurled it into the water. It hit the surface with a satisfying *plunk!* A small column of water rose into the air, then settled, sending ripples across the still waters of the river's surface.

His phone chimed. It was Gabi.

*Leaving Dallas in the morning for Ruidoso. Can't wait to see you there!*

Matt smiled. *Me either!*

He walked to the front of his truck and climbed in, heading north for New Mexico.

# 9

RUIDOSO, NEW MEXICO IS a mountain town known as a vacation spot. Just north of the city is the historic town of Lincoln, one of the main locales of the Lincoln County War fought by Billy the Kid, among others. To the east is Roswell, known for the alien landing.

Gabi and Matt didn't explore much. As soon as they got to town, they disappeared into a hotel room.

***

"What happened to your ring?" Gabi asked Wednesday morning.

They were spooning, Matt's hands on her bare breasts.

"Decided to get rid of it," he replied.

"Oh? You didn't like it?"

"I didn't like the accessories," he said.

"The clown?"

"Yeah, wait…" Matt thought about the time they spent together. "How'd you know about that?"

"Garrett." She rolled over to face him. "He thought you were going nuts."

"Jesus. So his solution was to tell the woman I've wanted since I met her."

Gabi shrugged. "Hey, it worked, didn't it?"

"It did." Matt leaned in and kissed her.

"You think without the ring, the clown won't show up?"

Matt shrugged. "I guess we'll find out tonight." He kissed her neck, drawing a laugh, then a moan. "At least I still have the luck."

"You never needed luck, you idiot," Gabi replied, lifting his head to kiss him on the mouth.

***

"I'd ask if you're rested, but I know better," Garrett said.

"Thanks, man."

Garrett shook his head. "Look, if someone has to bone my sister, it might as well be someone I like."

"And you're hoping I see it the same way?"

"Well…yes…"

Matt laughed. "Kaci's engaged."

Garrett's mouth dropped open. "Where's that fucking ring?" he said when he finally recovered.

"Bottom of the Pecos River," Matt replied as they walked toward the rodeo office. "I decided the clown wasn't worth it."

"Well, shit, you could have given it to me! Maybe I thought the clown was worth it!"

Matt looked at the notice pinned to the board. "You got *Trifecta.* Ain't he the one that threw you over the fence at Dodge City?"

"Right into the arms of a beautiful woman—surrounded by her husband and five brothers," Garrett confirmed. "Couldn't even steal a kiss with that bunch watching."

"Looks like I've got *Revenuer* again," Matt said.

Garrett shook his head. "Jesus, I hate your luck."

★★★

*Trifecta* didn't throw Garrett over the wall, but the bull did send him to the dirt before the horn sounded. To add insult to injury, he tossed Garrett before he could get clear, using his horns to throw him in the air. Garrett got up holding his arm.

"You okay?" Matt asked when he got behind the chutes.

"No," Garrett winced. "It's broken, sure as hell."

Gabi appeared. "Need me to take you to the hospital?"

Garrett nodded. "Please."

"Want me to go too?" Matt asked.

Garrett shook his head. "Not unless your bull sends you."

"Good luck," Gabi told Matt, leaning over to kiss him. "I'll see you later."

"Jesus," Garrett muttered as they walked away. "A broken arm and nausea…"

"Did you want two broken arms?" Matt heard Gabi ask as he headed toward the chutes.

★★★

*Revenuer* was as stoic in the chute as he had been at Pecos. He barely moved as Matt finished making his adjustments.

The grandstands were full, with locals and tourists coming together to watch the rodeo. Matt looked out through the bars in the gate, relieved he didn't see Turquoise the Clown, and got set.

Then he nodded.

*Revenuer* exploded out of the chute, starting a leaping spin that tested Matt. The bulls were as much athletes as the riders, something that was often said but not always appreciated.

This bull was a young Michael Jordan.

He came out of the spin and twisted, then took a leap that almost unseated Matt. *Revenuer* turned again, then went into his leaping turn as the horn sounded.

Matt slid off and punched the air as the bull moved away. He ran for the chute, climbing inside and pulling off his helmet to wave to the cheering crowd.

A minute later, the announcer's voice boomed through the speakers. *Matt McAllister on Revenuer with a 94 point ride!*

The crowd roared their approval and Matt raised his hat again in acknowledgement.

*Who needs that fucking ring,* he thought. *I've got all the luck I need!*

★★★

An hour later, he let himself into the hotel room. Gabi had texted, telling him Garrett had been right: a broken bone and no need for him to come to the hospital.

Matt flipped on the light and froze.

The bed was made, except for a single pillow sitting in the middle of it.

On that pillow was the ring.

# 10

"WHERE DO YOU THINK it came from?" Gabi asked.

She was sitting next to Matt on the bed, studying the ring. He'd sat there an hour before she came in, and now they were contemplating it together.

"I know where it came from," Matt chuckled. "The bottom of the Pecos River."

She rolled her eyes. "Okay, smartass, how did it get here?"

"That's the question," Matt said.

"If my brother hadn't been in Amarillo, I'd say it was his idea of a joke."

Matt nodded agreement. "But he didn't know I got rid of it until he got here."

A knock at the door made them both jump. Matt went and looked out the peephole. "Speak of the devil."

Garrett came in wearing a sling. "You don't look so hot, future brother-in-law. You better not give Sis any disease…" His voice trailed off when he saw the ring on the bed. "I thought you said you threw that in the river?"

"I did."

"Shit." He stood beside the bed, looking down at it. "Are you sure it's the same ring?"

"I don't know how it couldn't be. I've never seen anything else like it." Matt picked up the ring, studying it.

"You said the lady at the museum told you it belonged to someone named 'Turquoise the Clown?'" Gabi asked.

Matt nodded. "He died during a performance at Silver City."

"I'd say maybe he didn't want the ring to leave Pecos," Garrett said. "Like in all those scary movies."

"But if that's the case, why bring it all the way up here to Ruidoso?" Gabi asked. "The bottom of the river is closer to Pecos."

"Unless it isn't Pecos." Matt reached for his computer.

"What are you looking for?" Gabi asked.

"Turquoise's obituary."

It took him a few minutes, but he finally said, "I got it. He's not buried in Pecos. They buried him in Silver City."

"You think he wants the ring back?" Garrett asked.

"He's dead, I don't know what he wants," Matt said. "But it's as good a guess as any. That or he plans to keep showing up until he finally does something to make a bull kill me."

"I hope not," Gabi said.

Matt shook his head. "I don't know why I said that. He obviously wants me alive."

"He better." Gabi reached over and squeezed his hand.

Garrett rolled his eyes. "Would you two get a room?"

"We did," Matt shot back. "You're standing in it."

A shake of the head. "Whatever, man. So I guess you'll be wanting to get up bright and early so you can return this ring before the rodeo tomorrow night?"

Matt looked down at the ring and nodded. "Yeah. Let's get this over with."

★★★

Silver City, named for the mineral found in the mountains around the settlement, is in the western part of New Mexico. Nestled in a narrow valley, the town had grown from its frontier roots to host a college. Billy the Kid's mother is buried in the town cemetery.

Turquoise the clown wasn't.

He was buried in a small cemetery on the western slope of the valley, overlooking the town.

"I'm glad I'm not the gravedigger," Garrett said as they climbed out of Matt's truck. "This is solid rock."

Matt nodded, helping Gabi out and taking her hand.

The cemetery was surrounded by a chain link fence. There were only a handful of graves, granite markers identifying them.

"Spread out," Garrett said. "We'll cover more ground that way."

"Who are we looking for?" Gabi asked.

"Turquoise the clown," Garrett replied.

"No, what's his real name?" Gabi looked at Matt, who shrugged.

"I don't remember."

She rolled her eyes. "Did you two seriously think you'd just walk in here and find a grave marked 'Turquoise the Clown?'"

Matt and Garrett looked at each other.

"Okay," Garrett said, "so we may have fallen off a bull or two too many."

Matt had his phone out. "Dewayne Smith," he said. "His wife is Sulema."

"Okay," Garrett said. "This shouldn't take long."

Matt was almost to the far corner of the cemetery when he heard Gabi call. "Got it!"

He walked along the fence until he reached where she was standing, looking down at a black marble headstone.

The letters were turquoise, and a slab of the rock had been mounted in the base of the stone.

*Dewayne Smith,* the left side read. *Turquoise the Clown.*

Matt took her hand and squeezed it. "What do you know, a grave marked 'Turquoise the Clown.'"

Gabi shook her head. "If you know what's good for you, you'll shut up now."

"He doesn't," Garrett said as he walked up and looked down at the gravestone. "I'll be damned…"

"Especially if you finish that sentence," Gabi shot.

Matt took the ring out of his pocket and placed it on the slab of turquoise on the gravestone.

"Is that it?" Garrett asked, reaching in his pocket for a bandana to wipe the sweat off his brow. "Kind of anticlimactic."

"I'll take that over seeing the clown again," Matt replied, studying the stone.

Gabi squeezed his hand. "Come on, let's get out of here. It's too hot to stand around."

# 11

Matt felt confident walking into the rodeo arena that night. The ring was gone, the clown with it, and he was ready to kick some ass. Gabi would be in the stands cheering him on, and afterward they'd head back to the motel to fuck like rabbits. Then tomorrow, they'd head for Santa Fe and do it all over again.

It was the kind of life he could love.

He stopped at the office to check the draw. *Nightmare Fuel*. A good bull, one he'd never ridden but had seen at a few other rodeos.

"Who was I gonna have?" he heard Garrett ask from behind him.

Matt checked the sheet again. "*Ocho Seis.*"

"Maybe this broken arm is a blessing. He threw my ass in Pampa last year."

Matt turned around, grinning. "I rode him just fine at Laredo."

Garrett flipped him off. "You've been riding a lot of things just fine lately."

Matt grinned. "Just because you didn't get a nurse's number last night is no reason to get testy."

Garrett rolled his eyes as they walked toward the arena. The sun was already sinking, and Silver City's altitude combined with it to make it cooler than their previous stops.

"I'm gonna go take a piss," Matt said, turning toward the hall that led under the stands to the restroom.

"Have fun."

Matt walked down the dark-ish hall, the fluorescent lights overhead just bright enough to see where he was going. When he got to the men's room, he looked further down the hall and saw a crumpled figure lying on the floor.

"Hello?" Matt called. "Are you okay?"

He walked down the hall into the shadows and knelt next to the fallen figure. It rolled face-up, and when Matt saw the turquoise paint on the man's face, he jumped back.

"You fool," Turquoise whispered. "I didn't want the damn thing back. I was trying to save you."

"Save me from what?" Matt asked, looking at the clown's injuries. He was equipped differently from modern bullfighters, without the protective gear that kept them safe in the arena. The clown's chest had caved in and blood had soaked his black shirt.

"Forty-two years ago, this tunnel led to the arena floor. When the bull got me, they brought me in here. I didn't last long, despite the doctor's best efforts. I died here in the tunnel, that damn ring on my finger."

"I know," Matt replied. "I saw the article."

"That article didn't tell the whole story," Turquoise gasped, red froth appearing at the corner of his mouth. "I found the ring in a pawn shop in Santa Fe. Thought it looked like a lucky charm, so I bought it. For a while, I had it all. My career took off, no more small potato circuits, I was working the big rodeos. Odessa, San Antonio, Houston, Dallas, Phoenix, Cheyenne. But the better it got, the more I wanted to believe I was responsible for my success, not a hunk of metal. So I tossed it in the Rio Grande. That night, my ego caught up to me, here in Silver City. I got gored."

"Jesus," Matt whispered.

"I wasn't trying to scare you," the clown whispered. "I was trying to warn you. The ring is lucky, but it makes you a slave. When I took it off, my skin was discolored, like the ring was still there. I may have let go of it, but it wasn't done with me."

Matt looked down at his hands. His finger looked the same as it always had, nothing discolored or looking like the ring.

Turquoise opened his hand, revealing the ring. "It hasn't bonded into you the way it did me. I guess that's another way you're lucky. You've got a choice to make, Kid. Wear the ring, keep your luck, but know that one day, your ego will be your downfall. Or walk away now, take what you have, and live with the same luck as everyone else."

"What happens to the ring?" Matt asked.

"If you don't take it?" A shrug. "Maybe it dies with me. I hope it dies with me."

Matt didn't hesitate. He closed the clown's bloody fingers around the ring.

"Good choice, cowboy," Turquoise whispered, then laid down on the hard concrete and closed his eyes. As his body relaxed, his fingers opened, revealing that the ring had vanished.

A wave of relief washed over Matt. This time, he realized, the damn ring was gone.

***

The first two riders failed to qualify.

As Matt settled into the chute, positioning himself on *Nightmare Fuel,* he wondered how tonight would go without his lucky charm. He wrapped the rope around his hand carefully. The bull was nervous, stepping in the stall, but not babying Matt into the sides.

The announcer was working the crowd: "*I know you came here tonight to see a qualified ride, but to make that happen, you gotta get loud for these cowboys! Let them hear you, and they'll give you everything they've got!*"

Matt looked out and saw Turquoise standing in the middle of the arena, blood covering the front of his clothes from the hole in his chest. When he saw Matt looking at him, he winked, then disappeared.

Garrett reached down to squeeze his shoulder. "You got this, bud."

A smile crossed Matt's face.

The ring was gone.

But he was still a cowboy.

Matt took a deep breath and nodded.

The gate slammed open.

# Acknowledgements

Thank you to:

Chloe York for her editing expertise. She took a book I thought was pretty good and helped me make it better than I could have hoped.

Christy Aldridge with Grim Poppy Designs for the amazing cover.

All of the ARC Readers and Reviewers (you know who you are!).

Wednesday for doing her best to add typos to the manuscript.

Atlas for staying out of the way and

watching YouTube.
Anna for all the love.
And you, dear reader, for reading this work!

# About the author

D.L. WINCHESTER LIVES IN *the foothills of southern Appalachia. A former mortician, his work searches the darkness to find tales worth telling. He is the author of over three hundred obituaries, numerous short stories, the novellas* The Screaming House *and* Devil's Fork, *several novelettes, and the collections* Shadows of Appalachia *and* A Terrible Place and Other Flashes of Horror.

*D.L. also serves as the President and Associate Editor of Undertaker Books, an independent horror publisher. In his spare time, he can be found searching for inspiration in the world around him and helping his wife try to keep their children from becoming the next generation of horror villains.*

# Follow the Author

# Also by D.L. Winchester

*Shadows of Appalachia*
*A Terrible Place*
*The Screaming House*
*Devil's Fork*
*Dead Money*
*The Colony*
*Mother Clucker*
*Night of the Chupacabra*
*It Came From the Morgue*
*Night Shift*

*Return of the Mother Clucker*
*Rodeo Clown*